D1438083

PUFFIN BOOKS

Editor: Kaye Webb

A BOOK OF MILLIGANIMALS

What did the sardine's mother say when she saw her first submarine? – 'It's only a tinful of people.' And what is the difference between arctic elephants and the African kind? – Nothing, except they are colder.

This is the kind of entertaining zoological lore you will find in this new collection of Spike Milligan's inspired nonsense poems and drawings. If you liked his other Puffin, *Silly Verse for Kids*, you will love this one!

Cover design by Gerald Downes

A Book of
Milliganimals

BY

Spike Milligan

PUFFIN BOOKS

Puffin Books: a Division of Penguin Books Ltd,
Harmondsworth, Middlesex, England
Penguin Books Australia Ltd, Ringwood, Victoria, Australia
Penguin Books Canada Ltd, 41 Steelcase Road West, Markham, Ontario, Canada
Penguin Books (N.Z.) Ltd, 182-190 Wairau Road,
Auckland 10, New Zealand

—

First published by Dobson Books 1968
Published in Puffin Books 1971
Reprinted 1971, 1973 (twice), 1974

—

Copyright © Loan-out Ltd, 1968

—

Made and printed in Great Britain by
Cox & Wyman Ltd,
London, Reading and Fakenham
Set in Monotype Joanna

This book is sold subject to the condition
that it shall not, by way of trade or otherwise,
be lent, re-sold, hired out, or otherwise circulated
without the publisher's prior consent in any form of
binding or cover other than that in which it is
published and without a similar condition
including this condition being imposed
on the subsequent purchaser

Dedication

I'd like to dedicate this book to
Dr and Mrs J. Robson
for helping me during a sticky*
patch in my life.

*I used to be a fly

Contents

PART ONE

Animals

Three-legged Hippo

HIP-HIP- HIPPO!

THREE LEGGED HIPPO

Seated Position

RARE BACK
VIEW

Arctic Elephant

Arctic elephants are the same as African ones only they're colder. Feel one.

Moos

Highly trained Moo-Cows doing impressions* of Moo-Zebras.

Strawberry Moose

Leopards

Leopards are easily spotted.
Just fill in the white circles with black ink.

The Cheetah

A sleek cat is the Cheetah,
No other could look neetah,
He's heavily dotted . . .
So he's easily spotted . . .
And he lives in Tanganyika.

Pygmy Elephant

The Pygmy Elephant is made
Much shorter than the giant brigade.
He lives much closer to the ground
And that is where he's usually found.
Why should an Elephant be so wee?
My friend, it's no good asking me!

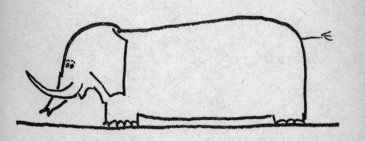

Alligator

From Sydney Zoo
An Alligator
Was put on board
A flying freighter.
He ate the pilot
And the navigator
Then asked for more,
With mashed potater.

Much later

Tiger, Tiger Burning etc.

Tigers travel stealthily
Using, first, legs one and three.
They alternate with two and four;
And, after that, there are no more.

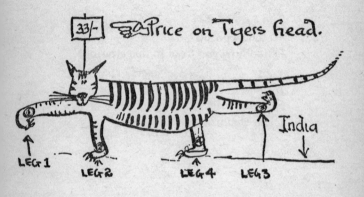

Envoi

Tiger, Tiger burning bright,
Look out! You'll set the jungle alight.

Ant and Eleph-Ant

Said a tiny Ant
To the Elephant,
'Mind how you tread in this clearing!'

But alas! Cruel fate!
She was crushed by the weight
Of an Elephant, hard of hearing.

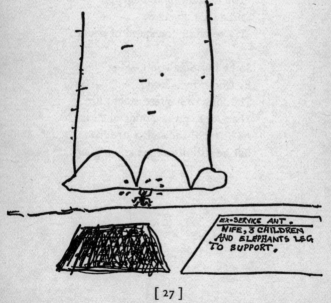

EX-SERVICE ANT.
NIFE, 3 CHILDREN
AND ELEPHANTS LEG
TO SUPPORT.

Silly Old Baboon

There was a Baboon
Who, one afternoon,
Said, 'I think I will fly to the sun.'
So, with two great palms
Strapped to his arms,
He started his take-off run.

Mile after mile
He galloped in style
But never once left the ground.
'You're running too slow,'
Said a passing crow,
'Try reaching the speed of sound.'

So he put on a spurt –
By God how it hurt!
The soles of his feet caught fire.
There were great clouds of steam
As he raced through a stream
But he still didn't get any higher.

Racing on through the night,
Both his knees caught alight
And smoke billowed out from his rear.
Quick to his aid
Came a fire brigade
Who chased him for over a year.

Many moons passed by.
Did Baboon ever fly?
Did he ever get to the sun?
I've just heard today
That he's well on his way!
He'll be passing through Acton at one.

P.S. Well, what do you expect from a Baboon?

Giraffe no I

We come now to
   the stately Giraffe
Who's never been known
   to smile or laugh.

But once, long ago,
   he laughed at a Tory
Who told him, they say,
   a very tall story!

———

Giraffe no 2

This self-made Giraffe
Was mentioned in despatches
For making himself
With sawdust, string and patches.

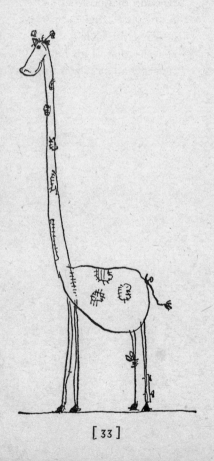

The Lion

A Lion is fierce:
His teeth can pierce
The skin of a postman's knee.

It serves him right
That, because of his bite,
He gets no letters you see.

AFRICA

The Pig

A very rash young lady pig
(They say she was a smasher)
  Suddenly ran
  Under a van –
Now she's a gammon rasher.

PART TWO

Milliganimals

A tourist who went to Tunisia
Said, 'Are we allowed to go fishing 'ere?'
  'Oh no,' said the Bey.
  'All the fish gone away.
I've only got chips on my dish in 'ere.'

Sardines

A baby Sardine
Saw her first submarine:
She was scared and watched through a peephole.

'Oh, come, come, come,'
Said the Sardine's mum,
'It's only a tin full of people.'

The Admiral Byrd

You must have heard
Of the Admiral Byrd
Who found a pole called South.

He flew all the way
From the USA!
Well Lawdy hush ma mouth!

Onecan

Toucans

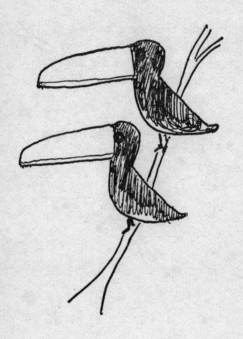

The Flea

How teeny teeny wee
Is the little tiny flea.
One would think that one so small
Could do no harm at all.
But all last night
In my hotel
He made me scratch
Like merry hell.

Words Said

'Bunga-louie lee!'
Said the monkey to the flea.
It wasn't much to say but —
It passed the time away.

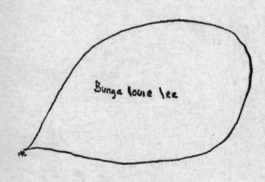

'Bunga-louie lee.' Word invented by Sile when popping a hand puppet around my bedroom door. She was about seven at the time.

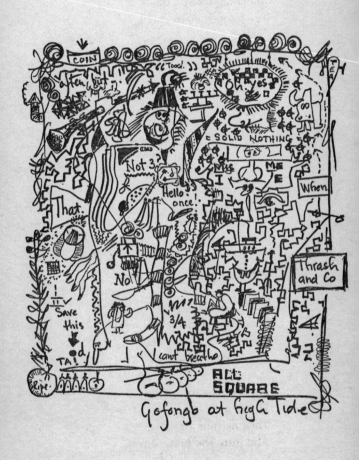

Gofongo at high Tide

The Gofongo, if you please,
Is a fish with singing knees
And a tail that plays
The Spanish clarionet!

He has toes that whistle tunes
And explode! Like toy balloons.
Hence his many,
Many visits to the vet.

The Gofongo, when he likes,
Swallows jam and rusty bikes,
Orange pips and treacle
Pudding boiled in glue.

He loves chips with rusty nails
And can swallow *iron rails*
That is why they cannot
Keep one in a zoo.

But! Gofongo as a pet
Would cause panic and regret.
People tried it and were
Nearly driven balmy.

For, once inside a house,
He screams, 'I'm a Jewish mouse.'
Then he runs away —
And joins the Arab Army!

Wiggle-Woggle

The Wiggle-Woggle said,
'When I'm standing on my head
I can see the coast of China
And it's very, very Red.'

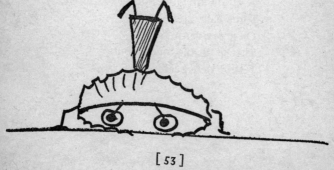

What the Wiggle-Woggle said

The Wiggle-Woggle said,
'I wish that I were dead:
I've a pain in my tummy and
It's travelling up the bed.
I wish that I were something
That never got a pain;
A little bit of fluffy stuff
That vanished down the drain.
I could be a tiger's whisker,
A tuba made of bread,
The purple eye
Of a custard pie
With a trouser made of lead.
There must be other somethings —
A tiny leather bead?
Or a bit of crumpled paper
Where the water-melons feed?
A yellow thing with lumps on!
A yellow thing without!!
Some hairy stuff
On a powder puff
That snuffs the candles out.
Wish I were a lamp post

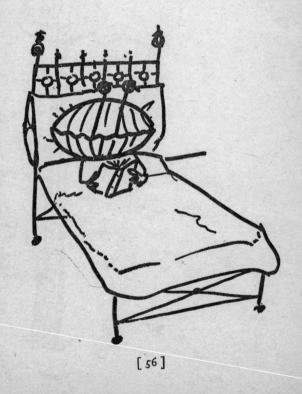

(Lamp posts don't get pains),
A leaky rusty gutter
Flooding other people's drains!
All *those* are what I'd like to be,'
The Wiggle-Woggle said.

But he stayed a Wiggle-Woggle
And, what's more, he stayed in bed!

PART THREE

The sad happy ending story of
The Bald Twit Lion
A story for very all ages

Once, twice and thrice upon a time there lived a Jungle. It started at the bottom and went upwards till it reached the monkeys, who had been waiting years for the trees to reach them, and as soon as they did the monkeys invented climbing down. Most trees were made of wood, and so were the rest. Trees never spoke, not even to each other, so they never said much (actually one tree did once say 'much' but nobody believed him), they never said 'fish' either, not even on Fridays. It was a really good Jungle: great scarlet lilies, yellow irises, thousands of grasses all grew very happily, and this Jungle was always on time. Some people are always late, like the late King George V. But not this Jungle.

This Jungle became very, very popular with lots of wonderful animals; there was absolutely no shortage of them and therefore the Jungle was ever so busy. This Jungle was called the Bozzollika-Dowser Jungle. Because. There was no organization there, but *everything* worked out perfectly. Some scientists tried to make an organized Jungle of plastic, but it didn't improve conditions and the scientists left saying, 'Let's go to the moon instead,' and as there is nothing on the moon it seemed the best place for them. Men kept coming to the Jungle looking for gold, diamonds, gas and oil. Whereas simple animals could live without the things, brilliant man couldn't, in fact he'd forgotten how to. One thing he never forgot was how to have wars and say, 'Oh dear, how sad,' when children were killed by bombs. The animals left these things called men alone. In return for this kindness man killed them, cut off their skins and put them on the floor; cut their heads off and stuck them on the walls. But if ever an animal killed a man, it was in *all* the newspapers.

But this story is a hap-hap-happy story, about animals. One day in the middle of the Jungle, near a village called Pongoland, a big lion called Mr Gronk had an attack of strongness. He was twenty-one that day and had been given the key to the Jungle, so he put on a fierce look and then, leaping in the air, he gave the biggest, loudest roar in the world. 'ROAR – ROAR ꝶ̊ꙍꜽ꛰ꞁꞮ ꝶ̊ꙍꜽ꛰ꞁꞮ꛰ ' he went; in fact he roared so loud that it loosened all the roots of his hair and tinkle tinkle all his lovely mane fell off, and landed on the ground PLIP-PLAP-PLOP 200,000 times, one for every hair. Suddenly Mr Gronk the lion saw himself in the Daily Mirror and, oh! he saw that he was now bald! A *Bald* Lion? 'Oh dearie me, I'll be the laughing stock of the hyenas,' he said. So he un-roared, ' ꞧꜽꙍꝶꞁ꛰ꞧꜽꙍꝶꞁ꛰ꞧꜽꙍꝶꞁ꛰ ', but his hairs didn't go back in, they just lay there smiling up at him, in hairy (that's hair language). Poor Mr Gronk, he now looked like a bald twit lion. As a passing hippopotamus said, 'I am a passing hippopotamus,' and went on to say, 'you look like a bald hairless twit lion.' When the lion heard that, he became naughty, angry and was just about to do a BIG roar, but no! he stopped, just in time; he'd better not roar any more, or something else might drop off him! He would look even sillier as a one-legged bald hairless twit lion, so, from then on when he was angry, he could only say

He roared so loud it loosened all the roots of his hairs and they fell out.

Monkey involved in Bald Twit Lion story. Also cashier at Zoo.

A Hippochondriac who was too ill to appear in the Bald Twit Lion story. So . . .

He would have looked even sillier as a one-legged bald twit lion.

very quietly, 'Tsu-tsu-tsu', and there is nothing funnier than a bald hairless twit lion called Mr Gronk leaping about the Jungle going, 'Tsu-tsu-tsu'.

One night when he was having tea (Lyons) he said, 'I can't go on being bald. It's a big problem: I must find a solution.' So he squeezed every tube in the Jungle but not one had the right solution in it. Then he thought, 'I'll try straining very hard and think about growing hairs.' So he strained, *strained* and STRAINED, but it only made his eyes water and his nose bleed. Everyone laughed. His own

Bald Twit Lion leaping and saying, 'Tsu! Tsu!'

Part time hairy ant eater
sitting on bald lions head

Part time hairy ant-eater
sitting on bald lions head.
for the second time.

flea left him. 'There's nowhere to hide on a bald twit lion,' he said and hopped it. He bribed a part-time hairy ant-eater to sit on his head; it really looked like real hair, but the lion got hick-ups and, each time, hairy ant-eater fell off. 'I'm off,' he said (which was obvious as he'd just fallen off). Lion was heart-broken. 'Sad growls,' he said and then did what no lion had ever done before, not even in the Ark, he laid himself down on the World and cried. 'Boo-hoo, boo-hairless-hoo.' The animals, having no television, gathered around him to look and feel sad. 'He must have an upset tummy,' said a monkey's stomach. 'I would say he's had bad news,' said a teenage coconut. 'Rubbish,' said a daft penguin and his cousin. 'Lions never get bad news. No one can ever get near enough to tell them.' 'I think I know what it is,' said an owl from his bed. 'His great-great grandfather was a baboon who tried to fly to the sun, and he has just heard about it.' All the animals shook their heads, and some fell off. It wasn't a very good day for the Jungle or the animals. To make it worse a mole made a mole hill that turned into a mountain and hurt its back.

Teenaged Coca-nut.

Daft Penguin.

Daft Penguin's First Cousin.

The crow that stood on Bald Twit Lion's nose.

By now Bald Twit Lion had cried so much he ran out of tears, and had to drink two gallons of water, (one for each eye). Then off he went again. 'Boo . . . -hoo. Boo-

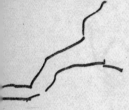

CHAPTER TWO

hoo.' All hope was not lost. A voice above him said, 'Please stop crying – I've got rheumatism and all this water doesn't help.' It was a lovely cross-eyed white crow (he had once been a black one, but he went colour blind making a rainbow). 'Things could be worse,' said Crow. 'You could be a Hamlet pencil, 2B or not 2B . . .' 'Oh, shut up,' said Lion. 'You're even making my misery miserabler.' 'Listen,' said the Crow landing on Lion's nose. 'Why don't you get all the other lions to shave their

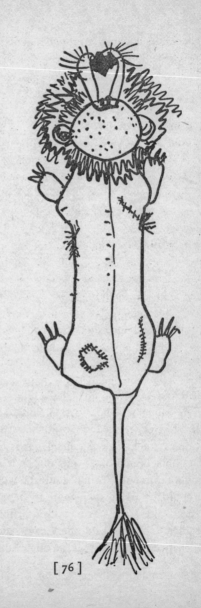

heads bald then yours wouldn't notice!' Bald Twit Lion
jumped to his paws. 'Whoopee! Saved! I've been saved.
Mr White Crow, thanks,' and he gave Crow a piece of
knotted string as a present. Round the Jungle raced Hairless Bald Twit Lion: 'Shave all your heads, or your legs
will drop off!' he shouted. Soon the Jungle was alive with
the sound of frightened lions shaving their heads to stop
their legs falling off. In fractions it went like this:

$$\frac{\text{Shave all your heads or your legs will drop off} = \text{fear}}{\text{shaving}} = \text{Bald Twit Lions.}$$

Next morning the Jungle was full of hairless bald twit
lions with legs and Mr Gronk was delighted.

So all that day the Jungle was a mass of leaping bald-
headed lions, all looking very pleased with themselves
for saving their legs. But, oh dear! Everything and every
non-lion animal burst out laughing. One monkey laughed
so much he fell out of his tree and krupled his blutzon,
but worse still, the lady lions were all furious with fury
at their silly bald husbands, so they refused to talk or
growl to them. All the bald lions realized they had been
spoofed. But then, along came a holy man called Daniel.
He took pity on them. 'Listen,' he said. 'I was once
locked in a den of lions, and none of them bit me, and the
audience asked for their money back, so it's my turn to
do you all a good turn.' So he did twenty good turns and
became giddy. Then he sat down, and started to invent

Monkey's view of Bald Twit Lion.

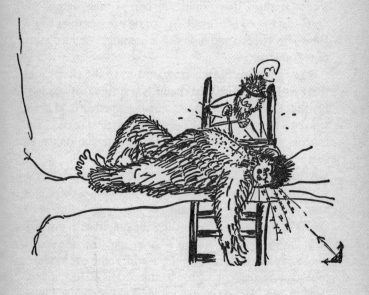

Daniel, snipping hairs of gorilla's chest to make lion wigs.

lions' wigs. He did it like this. After dark, Daniel would creep up to sleeping gorillas and snip-snip all the hairs off their chests. Daniel then stuck the hairs on a piece of rag, and glued them to the lion's head with nails, all except – Guess Who? Yes, poor old Mr Gronk the hairless bald twit lion. Because he was responsible for all the baldness, he was left out.

He became so sad he cried for forty days and forty nights and suffered from lakes on the knees. To make it worse there were ducks on the lake, they made such a noise at night he couldn't get to sleep so he got to wake. The quacking drove his knees deaf, in fact even if you hit stones at them they could not hear – they were stone deaf – and poor Mr Gronk had to tie ear trumpets to his legs so his knees could hear stones coming. What a picture of twit misery.

Now, you can't stop a story and leave Mr Gronk like that! No! He was still bald and it was this that changed his life. One day a party of tourists surprised Bald Twit, who was sleeping under a porridge tree for breakfast. The tourists couldn't believe their eyes, some couldn't even believe their teeth.

A bald lion? This must be the rarest animal in the world! Never in the history of the world had there ever been such a hanimule. It did not take long before great safaris of tourists were crowding the Jungle with cameras and flashlights. Mr Gronk's head became the most photographed bald head in the world, some people even took tape recordings of his baldness. His head got into the Top Ten Baldies; he out-balded Yul Brynner and Bing

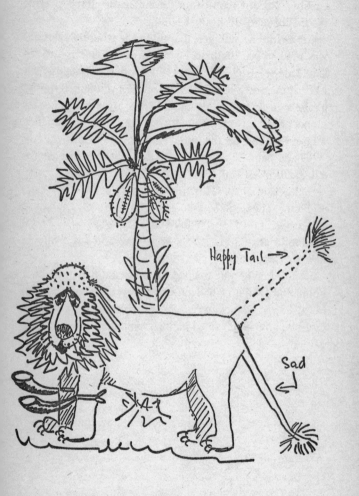

Happy Tail. →

Sad ↙

Poor Bald Twit Lion with deaf knees.

Crosby. Record companies even made long playing records of his bald head.

For a time he was very happy but – whereas everyone was mad to see his bald head, no one ever came to see him. This was the bitter end. But God was watching, he liked lions, so God slid down from Heaven on a religious giraffe's neck to the ground. 'Who are you, sir?' said Lion. 'I am Mr God. If you don't believe me, ask Giraffe!'

Lion did, and Giraffe said, 'Oh yes, he's God.'

'There,' said God. 'If you still don't believe me, ask me a difficult question.'

'O.K.,' said Lion. 'How much is 2×2?'

'Four,' said God.

'Oh yes,' said Lion. 'You're God all right.'

'Good,' said God. 'Close your eyes and say "Miggle Moggle Cake".'

Lion did. When he opened his eyes God had gone back home. But Lion now had a lovely lovely mane of beautiful black hair, and he was so happy he married a Roman Catholic giraffe and lived happily ever after until the next day.

End of Kid's book.
Start here for Grown-ups!

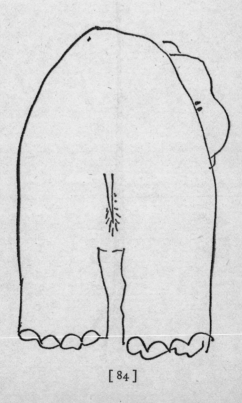

THE END

There are more than 600 other
Puffins to choose from, and some
of the humorous ones are described
on the following pages.

THE INCREDIBLE ADVENTURES OF
PROFESSOR BRANESTAWM

Norman Hunter

The Professor was a great (if absent-minded) inventor, always ready to turn his genius to the practical affairs of housekeeping, whether in the matter of a burglar trap or some comprehensive device to get spring-cleaning over quickly. His best inventions, however, seemed to land him in the worst scrapes, and somehow he never managed to solve the comparatively simple problem of keeping count of the five pairs of spectacles which he generally wore simultaneously, so as to be prepared for all eventualities.

PROFESSOR BRANESTAWM'S TREASURE HUNT

Norman Hunter

When it was a case of inventing an unspillable teacup, a collapsible-cum-expandable house, a liquid carpet to be applied with a brush, a machine for peeling and pipping grapes, a bomb or a fire alarm, Professor Branestawm was the man for the job. His interests were wide, and his intentions excellent, but it simply isn't any joke to be an inventor, or to be anywhere near one, as the Professor's military friend Colonel Dedshott and his long-suffering housekeeper Mrs Flittersnoop well knew.

Readers who first met this eccentric genius in The Incredible Adventures of Professor Branestawm will find the new adventures in this book just as hilariously impossible.

AUNTIE ROBBO

Ann Scott-Moncrieff

Life is full of surprises with Auntie Robbo. At eighty-one she can bound over the heather faster than most, and if some consider her mad, to her great-great-nephew Hector she is the only sane person in the world. When Merlissa Benck Murdoch descends on their household and announces her intention of adopting Hector, who could blame Auntie Robbo and Hector creeping off in the night and escaping to Edinburgh on top of a double-decker bus?

MY FRIEND MR LEAKEY

J. B. S. Haldane

Mr Leakey was the only magician who could bring a sock to life, or bewitch a tie-pin and a diary so that he could never lose them. He wanted to run over to Java after lunch, and was going to use a touch of invisibility in the morning to cure a dog that was always biting people.

If you want to know more about Mr Leakey and his household jinn and the octopus who served his meals and the dragon (wearing asbestos boots) who grilled the fish, you must read this book to find out.

For readers of eight and over, especially boys.

MIDNITE

Randolph Stow

Midnite was not very bright and so when he became an orphan his animal friends decided he should be a bushranger, but he wasn't very good at that either. He robbed a judge, and Trooper O'Grady robbed him.

A funny and unusual book, for readers of nine and over.

PATRICK KENTIGERN KEENAN

Mollie Hunter

Patrick Kentigern Keenan lived in Connemara, and he was a terrible boaster.

'I'm the smartest man in Ireland,' he used to say.

He had a nice wife called Bridget, and they might have lived very happily all their lives if Patrick hadn't tried to outwit the fairies. He cheated the leprechauns with false gold when they made him some shoes, and it's a brave man who tries to cheat them. In the end he is trapped with his little boy in a magic underground cave, with only one chance of escape. But he had got a magic chain, a golden spoon, a silver bridle, and an enchanted stone with him, so perhaps after all he was as smart as he said he was.

THE THIRTEEN CLOCKS AND
THE WONDERFUL O

James Thurber

The Thirteen Clocks is a mixture of fairy tale, parable, and poetry. It has everything in it to please everybody. There is a princess in distress, a prince in disguise, a wicked uncle, and a last-minute race between good and evil which is as exciting as any thriller. James Thurber wrote it because he couldn't help himself, which must be why it bubbles with gaiety and wit.

The Wonderful O is about two abominable villains, a man with a map and a man with a ship, who sail to the island of Coroo in search of treasure, and when they can't find it, revenge themselves on the gentle inhabitants by banning everything with an O in it. Illustrated by Ronald Searle.

HOW TO BE TOPP

Geoffrey Willans and Ronald Searle

It is only fair to admit that Nigel Molesworth, the Curse of St Custards, is not everybody's favourite character. There are masters who ban his presence in the school library, or cite him as an Awful Warning to their pupils, and there are parents who condemn his manners and his spelling as a disgrace to the noble name of Education. But there are also parents, the kind who treasure their children's first letters, who find him irresistible, and masters who use him as a valuable guide in the strange labyrinth of a Schoolboy's Mind.

A book for everyone over nine who wants to laugh and knows how to spell.

If you have enjoyed this book and would like
to know about others which we publish, why not
join the Puffin Club? You will be sent the Club magazine
Puffin Post four times a year and a smart badge
and membership book. You will also be
able to enter all the competitions. For details, send a
stamped addressed envelope to:

The Puffin Club Dept A
Penguin Books
Bath Road
Harmondsworth
Middlesex